THE SHEPHERD WHO SEARCHED

Written by Margaret Williams
Illustrated by Steve Smallman

CANDLE
BOOKS

Written by Margaret Williams
Illustrated by Steve Smallman
Copyright © 2006 Lion Hudson plc/Tim Dowley and
Peter Wyart trading as Three's Company

Published in 2006 by Candle Books
(a publishing imprint of Lion Hudson plc).

Distributed in the UK by Marston Book Services Ltd,
PO Box 269, Abingdon, Oxon OX14 4YN

Distributed in the USA by Kregel Publications,
Grand Rapids, Michigan 49501

UK ISBN-13: 978-1-85985-627-7
     ISBN-10: 1-85985-627-6

USA ISBN-13: 978-0-8254-7316-6
     ISBN-10: 0-8254-7316-0

Worldwide co-edition produced by
Lion Hudson plc, Mayfield House
256 Banbury Road
Oxford, OX2 7DH, England
Tel: +44 (0) 1865 302750
Fax: +44 (0) 1865 302757
email: coed@lionhudson.com
www.lionhudson.com

Printed in China

There was once a good shepherd who had exactly one hundred sheep.

He knew them all by name.
He counted his sheep every morning and night.

"One, two, three, four, five…
…97, 98, 99, 100."
All of them were safe in the pen.

Each day the shepherd led his sheep to a grassy meadow.
And found them clear water to drink.

The shepherd guarded his sheep.

He used his sling and his crook to
keep away wolves and foxes.

Each night he led the sheep back home.
He counted his sheep.
"One, two, three, four, five…
…97, 98, 99, 100."
All were safe.

In the morning he counted them again.

Then he led them to fresh grass and cool water.

One night he counted as usual,
"One, two, three, four, five...
...97, 98, 99..."
Oh no! He must have missed a sheep.

He started counting all over again.
"One, two, three, four, five…"
Still only 99!

Now the shepherd was very worried.
One of his sheep was missing.

The shepherd locked the 99 sheep safely in the pen.
He lit his lamp and set off to find the lost sheep.

He searched up high...
Nothing!

He searched down low…
Nothing!

He searched in muddy ponds...
Nothing!

He searched in prickly thorn bushes…
Nothing!

He walked for miles and miles and miles.

The shepherd grew tired and hungry.

"Baa."
He stopped and listened.
There it was again –
"Baa," more softly.

Could it be his lost sheep?
The shepherd hurried towards the sound.

It *was* the lost sheep!
The shepherd pulled his sheep from
the bush where it was stuck.
The little sheep's woolly coat was torn.

The shepherd gently carried
the lost sheep home.

When he reached the sheep-pen, he counted.
"One, two, three, four, five…
…97, 98, 99, 100."
All were safe in the pen again.

Then the shepherd went
off to find his friends.
"Come and celebrate!" he said.
"Because I've found my sheep that was lost."

The Bible says Jesus is the Good Shepherd.

God is happy when Jesus finds lost people
and they follow him.

You can read this story in your
Bible in Luke 15:1–7